SUMMER days and summ
border terriers Flip and Flc

Their human knowledge
they learn to cope with a cι
gentleman who believes that dogs should
be seen and not heard, and come to the
rescue when their young owner's face
turns a terrifying red after a morning at
sea.

Luckily, Bella, the friendly
neighbourhood dog, is always at hand
with helpful advice ...

TONY HICKEY is one of Ireland's most
popular children's authors. He has written
several plays for radio and adapted many
Irish novels for radio transmission.

This is his second Flip and Flop book.
For The Children's Press he has also
written the 'Matchless Mice' series of four
books, and *The Black Dog*, an adventure
story set in his home town of Newbridge,
County Kildare.

GW00858699

TONY HICKEY

more about
Flip'n'Flop

Illustrated by
MARIA MURRAY

THE CHILDREN'S PRESS

First published in 1992 by
The Children's Press
45 Palmerston Road, Dublin 6
Reprinted 1994

ISBN 0 947962 73 5

Origination by Computertype
Printed by Colour Books Limited

*For Kitty and Don and Roy
– in whose garden it all started*

Contents

1
A New Day Starts

Flip and Flop lay under a large bush at the bottom of the garden. Catriona, the cat, appeared on top of the garden wall and looked down at them. 'So there you are,' she said.

Flip and Flop growled by way of reply. They didn't like cats.

They had met Catriona one morning at the vet's. She had been in a basket, making loud, moaning noises. The dogs had never expected to see her again after they had gone back to the cottage in the Wicklow Mountains where they lived with Frank Johnson.

Then there had been a terrible flood. Part of the cottage fell down. Frank decided that they could no longer go on living there. He had taken Flip and Flop to his parents' house on the side of a hill overlooking the sea outside Dublin.

To the dogs' great surprise, on their very first day, Catriona had appeared on top of the wall and spoken to them just like she had this morning.

Life in the Johnson house was very different to living in the mountains.

There were gardens instead of fields and cars instead of sheep. But going for walks was just as exciting. Harry and Joan, Frank's younger brother and sister, knew all the short cuts and secret ways in the neighbourhood.

Bella, the wise old dog who lived next door, often came with them. She would run on ahead and find special smells and wild animal tracks. The fact that they never saw any of the animals who made the tracks didn't matter at all. It was being out for a walk that was important.

Following Bella through the long grass on the rough ground, or dashing through the undergrowth on the hill, gave Flip and Flop the same feeling of excitement they had got when they had first seen sheep in the Wicklow Mountains.

Left to themselves, they would have chased those white, woolly creatures. However, Frank had made it clear from the start that they would get into trouble if they chased sheep.

Only trained sheep-dogs were allowed near these animals. Untrained border terriers, like Flip and Flop, had to stay far away.

Flip sometimes still dreamed of sheep. He would dream that a great flock of them was coming towards him. He'd whimper and bark in his sleep until Flop would give him a nudge and say, 'You'll wake everybody up!'

What Flop really meant, when he said this, was that Flip might wake up Mr. Johnson, Frank's father.

One of the first things Mr. Johnson had said when Flip and Flop had arrived at the house had been, 'I don't want them peeing on or digging up my favourite plants.'

After that, the border terriers stayed out of his way as much as possible, even though he had later thanked them for warning Frank that the wall of the cottage in the mountains was going to fall in.

They had also done their best to remember not to dig holes in the garden. When they forgot, Mrs. Johnson, who was a lively, friendly woman, would go, 'Tut-tut, naughty, naughty,' and fill in the holes.

If she wasn't about, Joan or Harry would do it.

So far, Mr. Johnson hadn't seen any of the holes. Now he sometimes smiled and clicked his fingers at Flip and Flop. This could mean that he was starting to like them. But if Flop were to wake him in the middle of the night, he might become cross with them all over again.

Frank kept well out of Mr. Johnson's way too. He was writing a book and had given up his job in order to finish it. Mr. Johnson didn't think this was a very good idea. But Frank would not change his mind. 'It will take me only a few more weeks,' he explained to his mother. 'Then I can go back to being a teacher.'

Mrs. Johnson replied, 'You are old enough to decide things for yourself. Just don't upset your father!'

In fact, that seemed to be the one rule of the house that everyone who lived there had to remember: Don't upset Mr. Johnson!

'It's because he works so hard in Dublin,' Harry explained to Flip and Flop. He and Joan knew from the way that the border terriers behaved when they heard Mr. Johnson's voice that they were afraid of him.

'He has a lot of worries right now,' added Joan, 'but he's really a very nice man. When things are easier at his work, he'll be as friendly as can be!'

Bella didn't think that Mr. Johnson would

ever really take to Flip and Flop. 'It is like I told you that first day that we met. He doesn't understand dogs.'

That was why she always made sure that Mr. Johnson had gone to work before she came into the garden through a gap in the hedge.

It was for that same reason that Flip and Flop were now lying in the shade of the bush. In a few minutes they would hear the sound of Mr. Johnson's car roar up the drive. Once the car had gone down the road, the day could be said to really begin.

'Won't be long now,' said Catriona, flicking a paw at a butterfly.

'What won't?' asked Flip without thinking. Then he felt very cross with himself for letting Catriona know that he was interested in anything that she had to say.

'Before you two can come out of hiding,' Catriona replied.

'We are not hiding,' said Flop.

'Oh come now,' drawled the cat. 'What a fool you must think I am! Almost every morning since you came to live here, you rush down to this bush and hide under it until Mr. Johnson goes to work!'

'Just sheltering from the sun,' said Flip.

'And if the sun wasn't shining, I suppose you'd be sheltering from the rain,' the cat said.

'It hasn't rained for ages now, not since the flood in the mountains,' said Flop. 'Anyway, what has it got to do with you why we are lying here?'

'There's no need to lose your temper.' Catriona flicked her paw again, this time at a bumble-bee. 'I'm sure if I belonged to someone like Mr. Johnson I'd feel nervous too.'

'We do not belong to Mr. Johnson,' said Flop.

'And we are not nervous,' said Flip.

'Oh no, not much you aren't,' said Catriona. 'But I suppose you have more important things than Mr. Johnson to worry about now.'

'Such as what?' asked Flop. He didn't want to talk to Catriona either, but there was something about the way she said things that made it impossible not to ask her questions.

'Well, your walks, for example,' said Catriona. 'You won't get very many of those now that Harry and Joan are going back to school.'

Back to school? What did Catriona mean by that?

14

'You will have to rely on Frank to take you out. And we all know how easily he can forget things when he is writing his book!'

What Catriona said was true. There had been days when Frank seemed to have forgotten all about them. He'd come rushing downstairs late in the day and say, 'The dogs! I forgot to take the dogs for a walk!'

Mrs. Johnson would laugh and say, 'Don't worry. Joan and Harry took them out.'

But if Joan and Harry were off to some-where called 'school', they might have to depend on Mrs. Johnson for their walks! She was a very nice woman but not much fun to go for a walk with. She moved too slowly and always turned back just as the smells were getting interesting.

The glass door from the house on to the terrace opened. Joan and Harry came out and called to the dogs. Flop gave Catriona a smirk. 'No more walks with Joan and Harry, eh?' he said before he ran after Flip and began to jump around the two children.

Harry bent down and patted the little dogs.

Joan stroked Flop's ears. 'You should have been called "Silky" instead of "Flop". We are going to miss you.'

All the excitement went out of Flip and

Flop. They stared sadly up at Harry and Joan. 'We are going back to school today,' Harry said. 'That's why we are wearing these special clothes.'

For the first time, Flip and Flop noticed that the children were not wearing their usual jeans and tee-shirts. Instead, Harry had on dark grey trousers, a white shirt and a blue jacket. Joan was wearing a green frock and blazer and a funny-looking hat. 'They are our school uniforms,' she said. 'I go to St. Rita's. Harry goes to Rockforth. We have to be back by this afternoon. School begins tomorrow.'

Mr. Johnson came out to see what was delaying the children. 'Oh now, don't tell me you are talking to those dogs! They don't understand a word that you say except "food" and "walk". Your mother is waiting in the car. We will be late.'

'All right, we're coming, Dad,' Joan said. Then she and Harry both hugged Flip and Flop, went back into the house and closed the glass doors.

A few seconds later, there was the sound of Mr. Johnson's car driving away from the front of the house.

Catriona called out, 'Was I right or was

I wrong? Are Harry and Joan going back to boarding-school?'

Flip charged back down the garden. He felt very angry and very sad at the same time. The sadness was because Joan and Harry had gone away. The anger was because Catriona seemed to enjoy Flop and him being upset.

He jumped against the wall and shouted, 'You clear off from here! You're just a trouble-maker!'

Catriona was very surprised. 'Me, a trouble-maker? All I did was tell you the truth.'

'Yes, but you told it in a very nasty way,' shouted Flip.

'Leave her be,' a gentle voice said. It was Bella coming through the gap in the hedge. She had heard everything that had been said but had waited until the car had left before coming into the Johnsons' garden. 'She can't help the way she talks. Most cats can't. I'd have told you myself about the children going back to school, only I thought you already knew.'

'How could we have known?' asked Flop, who had made his way down the garden. 'And what exactly is a "school"?'

'It's a place where people go to learn things,' said Bella. 'Frank used to work in one. He was a teacher. Teachers help people to learn things at school.'

'And what is a "boarding-school"?' asked Flip.

'A boarding-school is a school where people live as well as learning things. Mr. and Mrs. Johnson often go away on business trips. They decided that it was better to send Joan and Harry to boarding-schools because of this.'

'And, as I said, when they are away there will be no one here except Frank to look after you,' said Catriona.

'You will both be fine,' said Bella. 'Frank would never leave you alone without food.'

'But what about our walks?' asked Flop. 'You know we are not allowed out by ourselves.'

There were two reasons for this. One was in case they got lost. Flip and Flop weren't too sure what 'lost' meant and kept meaning to ask Bella.

The second reason was in case they caused an accident by rushing across the road. They had soon understood what was meant by an 'accident'.

They were only allowed to run freely on the rough ground, on the hill and on the beach.

Of these three places, their favourite was the beach. They went there less often than to the other two places because it was the furthest from the house. But, oh, what a wonderful place it was and what fun it was getting there along narrow twisting lanes and down a steep flight of steps!

The lanes went between the gardens of other houses. There were always dogs in these gardens, who would rush to the fences and call out at Flip and Flop.

The first time they had seen the border terriers, they had called out, 'What kind of dogs are you?'

'We are border terriers,' called Flip and Flop. 'We come from Scotland. We are staying with the Johnsons.'

But now, with Harry and Joan gone away to boarding-school, it looked as though the days of the great walks were finished.

Then the glass doors to the terrace opened again. This time it was Frank who came out of the house and called to them. 'OK, you guys,' he said. 'Time for walkies! Bella, you can come too if you want to.'

All three dogs stuck their tongues out at Catriona. She gave a cat shrug and said, 'It's got nothing to do with me!' Then she jumped down to the other side and went off about her business while the three dogs ran to where Frank stood waiting for them.

2
The Beach

Bella, being older and wiser than the terriers, and not subject to the Johnson rules, did not wear a collar.

The three dogs and Frank walked up the drive to the front gate. Here Frank paused and looked up and down the road. Then, to the dogs' delight, he said, 'I think it is the perfect day to go to the beach.'

He took the same way as Harry and Joan always did along the lanes between the gardens. The usual dogs greeted them as they passed. A very fat Jack Russell called out, 'How can you go for a walk in all this heat! And who is that man?'

'His name is Frank Johnson. We were sent from Scotland to live with him,' Flop replied.

'Why has he never taken you for a walk before?'

'He *has* taken us for walks before. It's just that this is the first time he has taken us to the beach,' said Flop. 'Usually he is very busy writing.'

'The people I live with write too,' said the Jack Russell. 'Last night they wrote a very long note to the milkman.'

Bella gave a deep, chuckling growl. 'Frank writes books, not notes!'

'I ate a book once,' said the Jack Russell. 'I didn't like it very much.'

'Books are for reading, not eating,' said Flop. 'I thought everyone knew that!'

'Is there some special reason why he is taking you to the beach today?' asked the Jack Russell.

'The rest of the family are all out,' said Bella. 'I suppose he decided to get the walk over and done with before it gets even hotter than it is now.'

Frank, who had been thinking about what he was going to write after the walk was over, suddenly realised that the dogs were all talking. To him, of course, it was just loud barking. 'Be quiet,' he said. To the Jack Russell, he added, 'Scoot!'

The Jack Russell replied by saying in an even louder bark, 'This is my garden! I'll talk as loudly as I want to in it!'

But Frank just hurried on, not understanding. Fortunately, there was plenty of shade from the trees that lined the lanes so the

22

walkers did not feel too hot when they arrived at the steps down to the beach.

These steps were in the shade as well. There were very high walls on either side of them. 'Soon be there now,' said Frank.

The dogs did not need to be told this. They could see the pebbles on the beach and the sea sparkling in the bright sunlight.

Bella said, 'I might just go on ahead of you and see what's happening.'

Flip and Flop knew quite well that Bella was just not able to wait for Frank to make his way down the steep steps. She could smell the beach as well as see it and that smell was like no other smell in the world!

Somehow or other, Flip and Flop managed not to pull on their leads and walked a few inches in front of Frank. Then the last of the steps was reached. Frank removed the leads. Flip and Flop, like arrows out of a bow, rushed to where Bella was nosing around in the long grass that grew near the lifeguard's hut.

Soon the hut would be opened. The lifeguard would be on duty to help anyone who got into trouble swimming. A group of his friends would spend the day lying in the sun around his hut, talking and listening to music. By mid-morning, the first of the families would arrive to spend the day on the beach. By afternoon, the beach would be crowded. But right now, Frank and the dogs had it all to themselves.

Never had it been so full of wonderful smells!

Bella and the terriers dashed from one place to another. They sniffed and snuffled and dug holes to see what was under the smells. Then they smelt the most interesting smell that Flip and Flop had ever known.

'What is it?' asked Flip, ready to run forward to the pile of rocks from where the smell was coming.

Bella said, 'Be careful! A wise dog never takes chances. Watch what I am doing. Then do the same thing!'

Bella lifted her front, right paw and stretched out her neck. Her nose twitched. Then her ears. Then she stood absolutely still.

Flip and Flop did the same thing.

Then Bella changed paws and raised her left paw.

Flop got this wrong and tried to raise his left paw while his right paw was still in the air. He fell over on to the sand.

Frank had by now noticed the way the

dogs were behaving. He hurried over to them just as Bella moved a few inches forward followed by Flip and then by Flop, who wished that there was an easier way of not taking chances. He was also beginning to think that the strange smell was frightening.

'What are you doing?' Frank demanded. His trainers had made no sound on the sand. The dogs had thought he was still down at the water's edge, skimming stones out to sea. The sound of his voice startled them and made Bella forget all about being careful. She rushed forward to the rocks. There, in the middle of the rocks, was a huge sea-bird. Flies

buzzed around it.

Flop started to say, 'What's wrong with it?' but Bella and Flip weren't listening. Instead they were climbing over the rocks.

'No, you don't,' said Frank, grabbing both dogs by the scruffs of their necks. Quickly he put Flip's lead on Flip. Then he attached Flop's lead to the collar that Bella wore. He dragged both dogs away from the rocks and shouted at Flop to stay with him.

Bella and Flip twisted and turned but Frank went on dragging them along the beach.

Flop felt even more frightened as he trotted alongside them. 'What is the matter?' he whispered.

'It's the seagull on the rocks,' said Bella. 'It's dead.'

'What's "dead"?' said Flop.

'It's when you aren't alive any more,' said Bella. 'It happens when you get run over or very sick or very old. The seagull could have died out at sea and been washed in on the tide.'

Flip and Flop both knew about the tide. It sometimes came in right over the pebbles on the beach.

'But what were you and Flip going to do

with the seagull before Frank stopped you?' Flop asked.

'Roll in it,' Bella said. She sounded ashamed. 'It is something that a lot of dogs like to do. It goes back to the time when we had to hunt for our food. We would try and make ourselves smell like some other animal. That way we would fool the animals that we were chasing.'

'I never wanted to do anything as much as I wanted to roll on that dead bird,' said Flip. 'And I didn't even know why until now. Did you not want to roll on it as well?' he asked Flop.

Flop realised that he had wanted to, but falling over and feeling frightened had stopped him.

'It's a good thing Frank was with us,' said Bella. 'Imagine the trouble the three of us would be in if we went home smelling of dead seagull!'

'Ugh!' said Flop, and ran down to the water's edge to cool his paws which were very warm from walking on the pebbles.

Flip and Bella keened to be allowed to do the same thing. Frank said, 'All right, but no going back to the seagull!' He removed the leads. Bella and Flip ran to where Flop was skipping through the water. For the next ten minutes, they had a great time chasing each other in and out of the water.

Frank felt as happy as the dogs did. It was a long time since he had been down on the beach. He had forgotten how good it felt to walk by the sea when the sun was shining. 'I must come down here more often,' he told himself. 'It's a good thing to get out of the house.' Then he couldn't help wondering what the future would bring.

When he had finished the book, he would have to send it to the publishers to see what they thought of it. While he was waiting to hear from them, he would have to find a job and somewhere to live. He knew his parents wouldn't mind him living at home but it didn't seem right to him to do that.

Then there was Lucy, his girl-friend, who was acting in a film in America. It was she who had sent him Flip and Flop. She would be coming home soon. There were many things to be thought about. Then he heard someone call his name: 'Frank! Frank!'

The dogs heard the voice too and stopped playing to see who had called. At the far end of the beach, where tall cliffs came to the edge of the water, there was a white building with several rowing-boats close by. A man was standing by the boats waving. He called Frank's name again.

Frank waved back and said, 'It's Roy Andrews!'

As they got closer to the boats the dogs could see Roy more clearly. He was the same height and age as Frank and had a deeply tanned face. He and Frank shook hands.

'I thought I was seeing things,' Frank said. 'I thought you were living in South America.'

'And so I was until last week,' said Roy. 'But the job there finished so I decided to come home. But what about you? I heard you were living in the Wicklow mountains!'

'And so I was,' laughed Frank, 'until a few weeks ago. The cottage fell in. I'm back home until I finish the book that I'm writing.'

'You were always good at English,' Roy said. 'I could hardly spell my name.'

'That's not true,' said Frank. 'You just couldn't sit still long enough to try and write anything longer than a one-page essay. Anyway, we can't all be writers. You managed to get a degree in engineering and a job that lets you travel and see the world.'

'True. But it's great to be back home,' said Roy. 'Now who does this lot belong to?'

'The border terriers, Flip and Flop, are mine. Bella belongs to the neighbours.'

The dogs knew it was a waste of time to explain that they did not 'belong' to anyone. Roy and Frank would just think they were being noisy. They were glad they had not barked when Roy said, 'They are nice and quiet. I was thinking of taking one of the boats out to try and catch a few mackerel, like we used to do when we were at school.'

'That sounds great,' said Frank. 'But what do we do with the dogs?'

'Bring them with us,' said Roy.

Flip and Flop began to tremble with excitement. They were not sure what 'fishing' was, but a boat was the thing that Roy and Frank were pushing across the sand and out into the water.

Roy held the boat steady while Frank lifted first Bella and then the terriers into the boat. Then he and Roy climbed in, picked up the long pieces of wood called 'oars' and rowed away from the beach.

3
Fishing

When the boat reached the middle of the bay, Frank and Roy put down the oars. The boat bobbed around gently. The dogs were no longer trembling although Flop was not quite sure that he liked the way the boat moved beneath him.

Then Roy took two fishing-lines out of his pocket and handed one to Frank. Frank unwound it to make sure that it was not tangled. Then Roy gave him a squashed-up piece of bread with some meat stuck in it. For a moment, the dogs wondered if Frank was going to eat it.

Or, better still, give it to them.

Instead, Frank stuck it on the hook at the end of the line. Roy did the same with a second piece of bread. Then the two men threw the lines out into the water. The hooks sank.

The dogs stood up to see what would happen next.

The water was so clear that they could

see the hook with the bread far below the surface. Something moved and grabbed at the piece of bread.

'I've got something,' Frank said.

He pulled his fishing-line back into the boat. At the end of the line was a creature unlike anything Flip and Flop had ever seen before. They tried to sniff at it but Frank pushed them away. Bella said, 'It's called a fish. What Frank and Roy are doing is called "fishing".'

'Shhh,' Roy said. 'No noise!' Then he laughed. 'I've caught one as well.'

Frank threw his line into the water again while Roy pulled in the fish on his hook. Within the next few minutes, they caught six more fish. Then there was a long pause during which they caught none at all. 'We might as well take the boat back in,' Roy said.

'One more try,' said Frank. He swung the fishing-line around and around his head. When he let go of one end of it, it went much further out into the water than the dogs expected. Almost at once, Frank said, 'There is something at the end of the line! It feels like a really big fish!'

A really big fish! Would a really big fish

fit into the boat? Seagulls came rushing out from the cliffs to watch what was happening. They screeched and screamed so loudly that the dogs had to bark back at them. Neither Frank nor Roy told them to be quiet. They were too busy pulling the fishing-line back towards the boat.

Nearer and nearer came the fishing-line. The dogs could see a long, black shape attached to the end of the line. It stayed just below the surface of the water.

'Do big fish bite?' Flip asked.

'I don't know,' said Bella.

'What is it?' Frank was asking Roy.

'I don't know,' said Roy. 'I've never seen anything like it.'

The two men shaded their eyes against the glare of the sun. It was no longer possible to see the black shape. 'Maybe we should just let it go,' said Roy.

'We can't do that,' said Frank. 'It would be cruel to cut the fishing-line and leave the hook in the fish.'

The dark shape was only inches from the boat now. The dogs stood staring at it. They were too excited and frightened to move.

Frank carefully lifted the fishing-line out of the water. The long, black shape began to change. Roy roared with laughter. 'It's a hunk of seaweed! There was a storm out at sea last night. The seaweed got tossed about. That's why it is in the middle of the bay!'

'And that same storm must have washed the dead seagull in,' said Frank. He unhooked the line from the seaweed. The dogs leaned forward to watch it sink down, down into the water. Then Flip leaned too far forward and SPLASH! he was in the water himself.

'Help,' he yelled. 'Help! Help! Help!'

The water closed over him. He could hear Bella and Flop calling to him. Then suddenly he was back on the top of the water. The boat was close by. He was able to move towards it.

'Good old Flip,' said Frank. 'You can swim!'

'So this is what humans mean when they talk about "swimming",' thought Flip. 'It's really very nice.' He managed to say to Flop and Bella, 'Come on in! The water's lovely!'

Bella said, 'I'm too old for swimming.'

Flop said, 'And I don't think I'd be able to do it.'

Frank had different thoughts. Before Flop knew what was happening, he was picked up and dropped into the water. Like Flip, he was sure he would sink like the seaweed

had. Then he came back to the surface and found himself paddling along beside Flip. 'You're right,' he said. 'It is very nice.'

They swam around for a while watched by Bella, who felt as proud as if they were her own pups. Then Frank said, 'That's enough. It's too far to let you swim back to the beach.'

He and Roy reached out and dragged the terriers back into the boat. Then they tried to get out of the way as Flip and Flop shook the water off their coats.

'We are going to be as wet as if we'd gone swimming ourselves,' said Roy. But he didn't sound cross about it.

When Flip and Flop settled back down, Flop said to Bella, 'What will they do with the fish?'

'Bring them home, I suppose,' said Bella.

Flip looked at the fish lying in the middle of the boat. When they had first been taken out of the water, they had wriggled. Now they did not move.

'Are they dead?' Flip asked.

'Yes,' said Bella. 'Most things have to be dead before humans eat them. Frank will probably ask his mother to cook them for lunch.'

She was wrong about this. When Roy and Frank had pulled the boat out of the water and put it back with the others, Roy said, 'Why don't we go and see if the cafe is open? We could ask them to cook some of the fish and give them the rest for themselves.'

'That is a great idea,' said Frank. 'Mackerel should always be eaten while it is really fresh. I didn't have any breakfast. Everyone was so busy getting Harry and Joan off to school that I stayed out of the way in my room.'

'I only had a cup of tea,' said Roy. 'And all that exercise has made me very hungry.'

The dogs realised that they were hungry too. And thirsty. Especially Flip and Flop after swallowing salt-water during their swim.

The cafe was a white building close to the boats. Flip and Flop had often passed it without knowing what it was. Mr. and Mrs. Murphy, who owned it, came out to meet them. They were delighted to see Frank and Roy. 'I thought it was the two of you out in the boat,' Mr. Murphy said.

'We should have come and asked permission,' said Frank.

'I'd be grateful if you would next time,' said Mr. Murphy. 'But I wasn't really worried. I could see that you knew how to handle the boat. You have a fine catch of mackerel, not to mention a fine set of dogs.'

'We were wondering if we could have breakfast,' Roy said. 'Four mackerel for us and four mackerel for the two of you.'

'That sounds fair enough,' said Mrs. Murphy. 'There's a bowl up there on the shelf. Fill it with water for the dogs. Then I think you should come inside to the cool, especially you, Frank. You seem to have got a lot of sun.'

'I've been out in it less than an hour,' said Frank.

'All the same, you can't be too careful with your kind of skin. Look at the glare off the sea now and it is only ten past ten.'

The humans and the dogs looked out at the bay. The sun was so bright that it was actually hard to see the water.

Frank gave the bowl of water to the dogs. They drank eagerly from it. Then they lay in the cool shadow of the open door of the cafe and listened to the humans talk. The Murphys had known Frank and Roy for a long, long time. They had many questions to ask about what had happened since they had last seen each other.

Roy told them all about his adventures in

South America. Frank told all about his time up in the mountains and how Flip and Flop had been sent to him by Lucy.

'When does she get back from America?' Mrs. Murphy asked as she watched the mackerel sizzle in a frying-pan.

'Soon now,' said Frank.

'Then I suppose you'll be giving us the big day?' said Mr. Murphy.

'That depends on a lot of things,' Frank said.

Flip and Flop looked at Bella. 'What's "the big day"?'

Bella said, 'It means getting married. I'll tell you about it when we get home.'

By now, the fish were cooked and the cafe was filled with a most delicious smell. The Murphys had already had their breakfast so they saved their mackerel for lunch. But they drank tea while Roy and Frank tucked in.

The dogs waited patiently. Roy and Frank both saved scraps of the fish which they mopped up with bread and threw outside for them.

The dogs wolfed the scraps down. They were delicious. Flop said, 'I suppose in a way you could say we helped to catch these fish.'

'Of course we did,' said Bella. 'We helped by keeping quiet.'

It was now time to go home. They said good-bye to Roy and the Murphys and set off.

As they reached the last of the lanes, they began to walk more and more slowly. Even the shade of the trees no longer seemed cool. None of the usual dogs came to greet them. The world had become a hot, silent place.

Frank gave a great sigh of relief when at last he turned the key of the front door. Then he opened the glass doors on to the terrace. He and the dogs stood there and looked down at the bay. It now seemed strange to think that they had all been out on it in a boat such a short time ago.

'I'd better start writing,' said Frank. He went upstairs to his room. The dogs went back down to the bush at the end of the garden.

'What a great morning that was,' said Bella.

Flip and Flop agreed. 'Yes, it was. We learned about dead. We learned about fishing. And swimming. And ... and ...' But the two little terriers never did finish what they were saying. Instead their heads began to nod. Their eyes began to close. Suddenly they were fast asleep. Bella looked at them, and thought of when she was a young dog. Then she settled down to sleep, hoping that the day might eventually cool down.

4
Flop Needs Help!

The sound of the telephone ringing in the house woke the three dogs. The sun by now was very high in the sky. The bush had lost almost all its shade.

'We've been asleep for hours,' Bella said. 'I'd better go home. My people will be wondering where I am.' Bella's people were Mr. and Mrs. Rice. Their children were all grown up. They lived in a pretty house called 'Rosetree'. 'I think the two of you would be cooler indoors. See you later on.'

Bella slipped through the hedge. Flip and Flop ran quickly up the garden and into the living-room. The coolest place they decided would be the hall. Fortunately the door into it was open. They flopped down by the hallstand. They could hear Frank upstairs talking on the telephone.

'Bella never explained about getting married,' Flip said.

'We can remind her later on,' said Flop.

Frank called down, 'Is that the two of you?'

Then he said to whoever he was talking to on the telephone, 'No, it's just the dogs come back in from the garden. Yes, all right.' Then he hung up and looked over the banister at Flip and Flop. 'Don't get into any trouble now,' he said.

Flip and Flop stared back at him in amazement. Something terrible had happened to him since they had last seen him. His face was bright red. It looked almost as though it was on fire. Yet he didn't seem to mind, or maybe he didn't know!

He went back into his bedroom and began to type.

'What are we going to do?' asked Flop. 'He needs help.'

'Wait until Mrs. Johnson comes home,' said Flip.

'That might not be for ages and ages,' said Flop. 'Let's go and call on Bella.'

Now this was something that the terriers had never done before. Always it was Bella who came into the Johnsons' garden.

'Going into Bella's garden won't get us into trouble, will it?' asked Flip.

'Not if we are trying to help Frank,' said Flop, who was usually more nervous than Flip.

They went to the gap in the hedge and looked up at it. It was fairly high off the ground. Bella, being a tall dog with long legs, had no trouble getting through it. For dogs as small as Flip and Flop, it was more difficult. They would have to stand on their back legs and use their front legs to get a grip on the branches of the hedge.

Luckily the branches at that point were quite heavy.

Flip went first. He pressed down hard on the branches and pushed himself up and forward. He landed safely on the grass on the other side. 'Come on,' he said to Flop. 'It's easy.'

Flop tried to do the same thing as Flip. Since he was fatter, the hedge bent more underneath him. When he took his back legs off the ground, he seemed to go much higher in the air. He struggled to keep his balance.

'Jump!' said Flip. 'Jump now!'

Flop struggled to do as he was told. But, as he jumped forward, a branch caught under his collar. He was left dangling several inches above the ground.

'I'm choking!' he gasped.

Flip looked at his brother in horror. Then he heard Bella call from the Rices' house.

'What are the two of you doing? What brings you into this garden? You know you're not supposed to leave yours.'

'It's Flop,' Flip called back. 'His collar is caught on a branch! He's choking!'

'Choking!' Bella was down the garden in seconds. She looked at Flop. 'Keep as still as you can!' Then, with a speed amazing in so old a dog, she ran back to her house and jumped and barked against the back door. 'Mrs. Rice! Mr. Rice! Quick!'

Mrs. Rice opened the door almost at once. 'What is this row about, Bella? Do you want to come in out of the sun?'

'No! No!' Bella said. 'No!'

Mr. Rice came to the door as well, wiping his mouth on a napkin. The Rices were having their lunch. He looked down the garden. 'It's one of the little terriers from next door,' he said. 'He's down there by the vegetables. Bella doesn't like him being there. She wants us to put him out.'

'I thought Bella liked the terriers,' said Mrs. Rice. 'I don't see why she would mind one of them being in our garden.'

'Of course I don't mind,' barked Bella. 'The terriers are my best friends. And Flop needs help. Please, please, follow me! Follow me!'

Flip shouted, 'What's keeping you? Flop could ...' and here he remembered the new word he and Flop had learned that morning on the beach, '... could be DEAD soon!'

Bella tugged at Mrs. Rice's skirt. Mrs. Rice said, 'She wants us to follow her. And the little terrier is trying to tell us something too.'

'Oh at last, at last they've understood,' said Bella as the two humans followed her down to where Flop still dangled from the branch.

'Oh the poor thing,' Mrs. Rice said. She held the branch while Mr. Rice carefully lifted Flop down. He ran his hands carefully around Flop's neck. 'He seems to be all right,' he said. 'But we'd better let Frank know what's happened.'

Mr. Rice, who was a tall, strong man, lifted Flop up as though he was a toy dog and carried him back to the house.

He put him down very gently on to the kitchen floor.

Mrs. Rice said to Bella and Flip, 'You are very clever dogs! The way you let us know that your friend was in trouble was great. Now just lie there nice and quietly with him while I telephone Frank.'

'And while I finish my lunch,' said Mr. Rice.

In spite of what had just happened, Flop

couldn't help being interested in what Mr. Rice was eating. However, Mr. Rice paid no attention to the three dogs. 'He never gives me anything off his plate,' Bella said.

'Neither do the Johnsons,' said Flip. 'They think it's bad for us.'

Mrs. Rice came back from the telephone. She looked very serious. 'Oh dear,' she said, 'I think I may have got the terriers into trouble! Frank was very cross when he heard what had happened. He said he'd come in at once to collect them.'

Mrs. Rice had barely finished speaking when the doorbell rang. She hurried off to answer it. Flip and Flop and Bella stuck their heads around the kitchen door so that they would be able to see for themselves how cross Frank was.

When Mrs. Rice opened the front door, she gasped in horror. 'Frank, your poor face!'

Frank, who had been ready to slap the terriers, said, 'What do you mean, my face?'

'Just look at yourself.' Mrs. Rice pointed to a looking-glass. Frank came slowly forward. His eyes opened wide. 'I look like a tomato with a wig on top!'

'Is it sore to touch?' Mrs. Rice asked.

Frank touched it and grimaced. 'Yes it is.

I hadn't noticed it until now.'

'Too busy with the book, I daresay,' said Mr. Rice who, now that he had finished eating, had come out into the hall. 'That's the worst case of sunburn I've ever seen.'

'I was out in a boat with Roy Andrews this morning,' said Frank.

'That's what did it so. The sun bouncing off the water.' declared Mr. Rice. 'If you ask me, it's the dog for the vet and you for the doctor!'

'Pay no attention to him,' said Mrs. Rice. 'I have some very good stuff for sunburn. Plenty of time to think of the doctor if that doesn't make it better.' She hurried upstairs.

Frank looked at the dogs watching him from the kitchen door. 'What do you think you're at, getting out of the garden? What would have happened to you if Mr. and Mrs. Rice hadn't been at home?'

'Oh now, all's well that ends well,' said Mrs. Rice, coming back with a tube of cream. 'And just think, if they hadn't come into the garden, I would not have seen how badly burnt your face is. In fact, far from causing trouble, they have probably saved you from having a lot of trouble with your face.' She handed the cream to Frank. 'Smear it all over your face right now.'

Frank did as he was told. The cream turned the colour of his face from bright red to pale pink. 'Thanks very much,' he said, holding the tube of cream out to Mrs. Rice.

'Keep it,' said Mrs. Rice. 'You'll need to put more on in a few hours' time, and again this evening and again before you go to bed.'

'I'll be like a grease ball by the time my parents get home! They telephoned to say that they were going to go for a long drive after leaving Harry and Joan at their schools.'

'Good,' said Mrs. Rice. 'Your mother is always sad when Harry and Joan go back to school. The drive will cheer her up. And it'll do your dad good to get out of the office.'

'I suppose so,' Frank said. 'Thanks very much for all your help. I'm sorry if the dogs were a nuisance.'

'No real harm done,' said Mr. Rice. 'But take this little fellow to the vet. And it occurs to me that it would be a good idea to make a proper gap in the hedge so that Flip and Flop could get in and out easily.'

'They'd be quite safe in here too,' said Mrs. Rice. 'They wouldn't be able to get out on to the road.' She looked at the two terriers. 'I wonder what brought them in here today.

50

You'd expect them to be worn out by the heat.'

'Yes,' said Frank. 'They seemed very tired when I brought them back from the beach. The last I saw of them they were lying in the hall.'

Mrs. Rice said, 'I have just had the strangest thought. Did they see your face?'

'Yes, they did,' said Frank. 'Surely you are not suggesting that they came in here to tell you that my face was sunburnt?'

'Well, I can't think of any other reason, can you?'

'No,' said Frank, 'but all the same ...' He looked at Flip and Flop.

Then he bent down and held his hands out to them. The two little terriers ran to him and licked his hands, which tasted strange because of the cream. But the dogs didn't really mind. The important thing was that Frank was no longer cross with them. They had been able to help him. And now there was to be a gap made in the hedge just so that they could visit Bella.

5
Cat and Dog Talk

At five o'clock, Frank took his car out of the garage and put Flip and Flop into the back. 'Off to the vet,' he said. Flip and Flop liked going to the vet. Dr. Neumann was always nice to them and there were usually interesting patients in the waiting-room.

It was also very nice to be able to look out through the back window at all the traffic and at the long lines of people waiting for buses to take them home from the seaside. The faces of some of these people were almost as red as Frank's.

'I wonder why they do it,' said Flip. 'I wonder why they lie out in the sun.'

'Beats me,' said Flop.

The car pulled in in front of Dr. Neumann's surgery and Frank put the leads on the dogs. 'Behave yourself now,' he warned as he led them up the steps. There were four patients there already. They were all dogs including Bran, the Irish wolfhound, whom they had met on their first visit there.

'Hello,' said Bran, who was lying at the feet of Brian, the boy he had been with last time. 'What brings you two back here?'

Flip and Flop told him the full story. The other three dogs listened as well. 'You 'ave 'ad zee lucky escape,' said a French poodle, sitting next to a woman with bright yellow hair. 'Such an 'orrible thing to 'appen.'

'Why do you talk like that?' asked Flip.

'It is because I am French,' said the poodle. 'France is a great country far across the sea.'

'We come from a country far across the sea too,' said Flop. 'We came from Scotland on a plane. Did you come to Ireland on a plane?'

The poodle looked very cross at being asked such a question. 'I do not remember.'

'Now, now tell the truth,' said Bran. 'You have never been to France. You were born right here in Ireland.'

'And 'ow do you know that?' asked the poodle.

'Because if you hadn't been born here, you would have had to go into quarantine and you would certainly remember that,' replied Bran.

'What's "quar ... quarantine"?' asked Flip, stumbling over the new word.

'It is a place where dogs from faraway countries have to stay when they come to live in Ireland,' said Bran. 'It's to make sure that they don't have anything wrong with them.'

'Sounds very lonely,' said Flop.

'Aye, that it is,' said a friendly-looking mongrel, whose human was a little, bald man. 'I met a dog once who had spent time there. He said he had never been so lonely in his life.'

'I am never lonely,' declared the poodle. 'We French poodles are too brave to be lonely.'

'But not too brave to be taken to the vet,' said Bran. 'What's the matter with you?'

'It is zee 'orrible red spiders,' said the poodle. 'I was taken on holiday to zee country. There was this wonderful big 'ouse with zee 'igh wall and all zee beautiful pine trees. Naturally I go and explore zee pine trees. What I did not know and zee 'umans, they did not warn me, was that there were zee red spiders in zee ground. They got into my paws. I think I go crazy. I am worn out from all zee chewing at zee itch.' The poodle held up a well-chewed paw. ' 'ow 'orrible to 'ave such a thing 'appen on zee 'oliday.'

The fourth patient, a spaniel, said, 'I got the very same thing last year. You have to have your paws dipped in special stuff. You'll soon feel better. I only hope that Dr. Neumann can clear up my stomach as quickly. I've not been myself all week.'

'Neither have I,' said the mongrel.

Flip and Flop found this very interesting. 'Who have you been then?' they asked.

The mongrel and the spaniel stared at

them. 'Are you making fun of us?' asked the mongrel.

'They mean no harm,' said Bran. 'They are still very young and don't understand everything. What gave you the upset stomach?'

'I think it was a bone I found by the bin,' said the spaniel. 'It smelled delicious and tasted delicious. But I felt as sick as a human later on.'

'With me, it was a dish of chicken and rice that was left over from Mr. Deed's dinner,' said the mongrel, looking at the little, bald man. 'He put too much pepper in it.'

'And what about you, Bran?' asked Flip. 'Why are you back here again?'

'Brian's young brother, Steve, ran over my front paw with his bike,' said Bran. 'It hurts me a lot.'

Just then, the door to the surgery opened. Dr. Neumann came in. 'Now then, who is first?' he asked.

'Cheeky is,' said the receptionist.

Cheeky was the poodle. He tried to look as dignified as possible as he followed the yellow-haired woman. All the same, he knew that the other dogs were laughing because he was called 'Cheeky'.

56

'Dear, oh dear,' said Bran, 'have humans no sense! The names that they give animals!'

'We were named after a pair of shoes,' said Flip.

By the time they had told the other three dogs the story of their time in the cottage, Cheeky was carried out of the surgery by the woman. He said, as he was taken to the outside door, 'Zee vet says 'e 'as never seen such a serious case. Or known such a brave dog! Long live France!'

The mongrel was next. Then the spaniel. In both cases, they were given pills and told to watch what they ate.

Bran, when he came back, had his foot bandaged. He limped after Brian to the door. 'It is not too serious. I have to rest to make it better. See you soon.'

Frank led Flip and Flop into the surgery and told Dr. Neumann what had happened. The vet examined Flop. 'He seems fine to me. *You* look as though you are the one who needs to be looked at.'

Frank was getting fed up with people talking about his face. 'I've put plenty of cream on it.'

'Put on plenty more,' advised Dr. Neumann.

Frank grumbled, partly to himself, partly to the dogs as he drove home. 'Such a fuss about a bit of sunburn! The cream makes it look worse than it is. If I had a tissue, I would wipe it all off.' He looked in his rear-view mirror at Flip and Flop. 'I still haven't decided if you tried to tell the Rices about my face. In fact, I think that I have been spending so much time at my writing that I can no longer guess what you are thinking. Now that Harry and Joan have gone back to school, I am going to take you out for a walk every single day.'

Frank could not have said anything that could have made Flip and Flop happier!

As soon as they were back in the house, Frank opened the doors on to the terrace. Flip and Flop ran to the big bush at the bottom of the garden to see if Bella was there. They wanted to tell her about their visit to the vet but there was no sign of her. She must be in her own house with the Rices.

'If Mr. Rice has made the gap in the hedge bigger, we could always go and visit her,' said Flop.

But the gap was still the same size.

'He will not make the gap any bigger until the fine weather ends,' a familiar voice said.

Catriona was back on top of the wall. 'It might hurt the hedge.'

Flop once more forgot about not wanting to talk to Catriona. He said, 'How do you mean, "hurt" the hedge?'

'By cutting it, of course,' said Catriona. 'If you cut a hedge very hard while the weather is hot, you could make it wither.'

'How do you know about the gap in the hedge?' was Flop's next question. Again he asked it without meaning to.

'Oh I hear things,' said Catriona. 'I heard about how you got caught on the branch earlier today. I am very pleased that Flip and Bella went to the Rices for help.'

Flip and Flop looked at each other. Did she really mean it when she said that she was pleased that Flop had been helped by the Rices? Or was she pretending?

'Oh I mean it all right,' she said, as if she knew what was in the terriers' minds. 'I am also very pleased that Mrs. Rice gave Frank that cream for his face. How did you get on at the vet?'

'We will not answer that question until you tell us how you find out what is going on,' declared Flop.

'I can tell you that very easily,' said

Catriona. 'Cats.'

'Cats?' said Flip. Once more, he found it impossible not to talk to Catriona. 'What do you mean by that?'

'All of us cats find out things and tell each other,' said Catriona.

'But there were no cats around when I got caught on the branch or when Mrs. Rice gave Frank the cream for his face,' said Flop.

'Are you sure?' asked Catriona in that slow, lazy, horrid way of hers. 'Are you quite sure that there were no cats about? Or do you mean that you didn't *see* any cats?'

'Is that not the same thing?' asked Flip.

Catriona gave a slight yawn. 'Of course it isn't the same thing. There are cats around your house and Bella's that quite often none of you notice. They sleep on the roof.'

'On the roof?' Flip and Flop stared up the garden at the house. It had a flat roof that the branches of a huge tree almost touched. It would be very easy for cats to climb that tree and then drop on to the roof.

As for the garden shed, a cat could easily jump off the wall and land on it. And there were at least seven window ledges at the sides of the house where cats could sit and listen to what was being said.

The branches of the big tree moved. Was there a cat up there right now? Was the outside of the house at this very moment covered with cats?

'I have to go,' said Catriona. 'There's a party down at the hotel. I said I'd be there. See you tomorrow.' She jumped off the wall. The dogs could hear her running through the long grass on the other side.

Then they stared at the house again.

Once more, the branches of the tree moved. This time Flip and Flop took no chances. They rushed up the garden and on to the terrace. They barked as loudly as they could at the tree.

Then they rushed around the sides of the house and barked at the window ledges, which were empty. Then they tried to see the roof of the shed but it was too high and the gate into the yard was locked.

Then they ran back around to look up at the big tree. Indeed they were so busy running and barking that they did not hear Mr. Johnson's car come down the drive. They got a great surprise when he came out of the living-room and yelled at them to be quiet.

'Disturbing the whole place,' he said.

'You've got every dog for miles around barking!'

This was true. Every dog that could hear Flip and Flop was calling out, 'What's wrong? What's wrong?'

'Cats on the roof!' Flip yelled back, forgetting about Mr. Johnson.

Bella, from next door, shouted back, 'There are no cats on your roof! I can see the roof of your house from our kitchen. There's nothing at all on it.'

'I said, "Be quiet!" ' Mr. Johnson yelled at the dogs.

'You're making more noise than they are,' Mrs. Johnson said as she came out on to the terrace. 'Where's Frank?'

'Where he always is,' said Mr. Johnson. 'Upstairs working on his book.'

'No, I'm not. I've come down to see what's upsetting Flip and Flop. It must have been the two of you coming home.' Frank walked across the living-room.

'They were kicking up a row before we got here,' said Mr. Johnson. Then his eyes changed as Frank came out on to the terrace. 'What have you done to yourself!'

'It's just a slight sunburn,' replied Frank.

'A slight sunburn indeed,' Mrs. Johnson

said. 'It looks terrible.'

'There's no need to fuss,' said Frank. 'Mrs. Rice gave me special cream to put on it.'

'I think you should see a doctor,' said Mr. Johnson.

'I've already seen a vet,' said Frank. 'I'll just have to stay out of the sun for a while.'

Flip and Flop plonked down on the terrace. What about Frank's promise to take them for a walk every day? Frank answered the question by saying, 'I will get up extra early every morning and bring the dogs out before the day gets too warm. Everything will be fine.'

'Well, I hope so,' sighed Mr. Johnson. He sat down on one of the chairs on the terrace and lit his pipe.

'What sort of day did you have?' asked Frank.

'A sad day and a glad day,' replied Mrs. Johnson, sitting on the chair next to her husband. 'It was sad leaving the children back to school. But I was glad that your dad took the day off from work. We went for a nice drive and had a lovely meal out. I'll get supper ready soon.'

'No hurry,' said Frank, sitting down to look at the view of the sea and the hills.

'It's a lovely evening now,' said Mr. Johnson. His anger at the dogs had gone. 'Frank, I know I've been hard on you lately. I don't want you to think that I am against you. I just don't want you to waste your time.'

'It won't be time wasted,' said Frank. 'The book will be finished very soon. I've asked John to look out for a job for me in London.'

John was Frank's brother. London was where he lived.

'That's a long way away,' said Mrs. Johnson. 'What about the dogs?'

'Oh we'll manage,' Frank said.

Then there was a great rustling in the branches of the tree. Flip and Flop rushed around the side of the house to have a look. There was no sign of a cat in the tree or on the window ledges. Flip called out as quietly as he could, 'Bella, any sign of any cats?'

Bella called back, 'I'll let you know if I see any.'

Flip and Flop came back to where the humans were. 'They seem restless this evening,' said Mrs. Johnson.

'It's the wind from the sea,' said Frank. 'When it blows, they go running.'

Frank's words made it possible for the dogs to lie quietly for a while. They knew now that it was the wind and not cats that was making the branches shake. And they also remembered what Catriona had said about the party at the hotel. Maybe all the other cats would be there too.

6
A Flying Bath?

Flip and Flop stayed out on the terrace while the Johnsons had their supper. There were several reasons for this.

One was because the dogs knew that they would never be fed at table.

Second was because the Johnsons were having salad for supper. Of all the food that humans ate, the dogs thought that salad was the least interesting. Harry and Joan had once saved them some and the dogs had hated it. They had spoken to Bella about it.

Bella had said, 'Salad is mainly eaten by rabbits and humans. Rabbits eat it because they know no better. Humans eat it because they think it is good for them.'

Flip had wondered if it would make the Johnsons' ears grow long and if they would start hopping around the place like rabbits.

Worse: Would Mr. Johnson, after warning Flip and Flop about digging holes in the garden, rush out and dig one himself?

Bella had asked, 'Do you mean a hole big

enough for all the Johnsons to live in? No, I don't think he will do that.' Then she shook all over as though she was laughing.

The third reason why the dogs went out on to the terrace was in case a cat should drop on the roof or climb on a window ledge.

They just could not help feeling somehow that this might happen, in spite of the cat party at the hotel. So while the Johnsons ate, Flip and Flop kept checking the sides of the house. They also kept listening in case Bella should call out, 'Cat on roof! Cat on roof!'

'It's a pity in a way,' said Flip, 'that the terrace of this house is not as high up the hill as the terrace of Bella's house. Then we could see for ourselves what was on our roof.'

Flop thought about this and about the way the Rices' house, in spite of being so close to the Johnsons', did look down on it. What Flip had said made a kind of sense. And, on the other hand, it made no sense at all. But, before Flop could decide what was right and what was wrong with what his brother had said, Mr. Johnson and Frank came back on to the terrace.

Mr. Johnson was smiling. Eating always put him in a good mood. He sat down and lit his pipe again.

Frank said, 'That's your second pipe this evening. I thought you were cutting down.'

Flip and Flop sat up straight. What was Mr. Johnson going to cut down? The hedge? Or the tree that touched the roof?

Mrs. Johnson called from the living-room. 'Frank is right. You are smoking far too much.'

Mr. Johnson was the only human that the dogs knew who smoked. At first they had been amazed at the sight. 'It's like a chimney in his mouth,' Flip had said.

'The smell from the pipe keeps the midges away,' said Mr. Johnson.

Frank swatted at the cloud of flies and moths that had begun to buzz around him. 'It's not doing a very good job.'

'It's that stuff that you have on your face that's attracting them,' Mr. Johnson said.

Then Mrs. Johnson gave a loud scream and dropped the plate that she was taking off the table.

Frank and Mr. Johnson, followed by the dogs, rushed into the house. 'What is it?' Mr. Johnson asked.

'It's a bat! A bat!' screamed Mrs. Johnson, running into the kitchen and slamming the door.

The dogs thought she had said 'It's a bath' and were truly amazed. They themselves hated baths but it had not occurred to them until now that Mrs. Johnson hated baths so much that she would break plates and scream and lock herself into the kitchen to get away from one.

But where was the bath? There was no sign of one in the living-room. Yet the dogs felt that Mrs. Johnson had not been talking about the bath upstairs.

'There it is!' Frank pointed to a high, dark corner of the room. There was a small shadow there. Suddenly the shadow moved and flew across the room to another corner.

'Don't start rushing after it!' Mr. Johnson said to Frank. 'Nip upstairs and get a bath towel.'

A bath towel! The dogs were even more amazed. Was Mr. Johnson going to take a flying bath? But how could he ever fit into such a small bath? And anyway, what kind of a bath flew?

The bath moved again; this time flying low over Mr. Johnson, making him duck out of the way. It made a faint squeaking noise but the dogs could not understand what it said.

'It can talk as well as fly!' Flip said. 'That

can't be right!'

He was about to rush forward and ask the bath some questions when Frank came back with a large bath towel.

'Switch on the main light,' Mr. Johnson said.

Frank did as he was told. The room filled with light. The flying bath turned in a circle. Frank flung the towel over it.

The towel fell to the ground, trapping the flying bath.

Frank carefully picked up the towel, took it out on to the terrace and shook it. Flip and Flop saw the dark shape fly off into the darkness at the end of the garden.

'Better close those doors,' Mr. Johnson said.

When Frank had done this, Mr. Johnson called out to his wife, 'It's all right. It's gone.'

Mrs. Johnson came out of the kitchen. 'Thank goodness that's all over! And please don't tell me that it was just a flying mouse. I've always hated them.'

'They're harmless,' said Mr. Johnson. 'People are afraid of them because they've seen too many horror films.'

There was a ring at the front door. 'Now who can that be at this hour?' asked Mr. Johnson.

'I'll go,' said Frank.

Flip and Flop followed him to the front door. It was Mr. Rice who had rung the bell. He was standing outside with a big stick in his hand. Bella was by his side. 'I heard your mother screaming and came down in case there was trouble.'

'A bat got into the house,' Frank explained. 'But it's very good of you to come down and make sure that we are all right.' Frank was trying not to smile at the thought of Mr. Rice using the big stick. 'Would you like to come in?'

'Oh no, thank you. Just as long as you are all right. I'd better get back. I arranged with my wife to call the police if I wasn't back within five minutes.'

'That was a very good idea,' said Frank. 'Oh and please thank her again for the cream. It's helped my face a lot.'

'You need to use more of it all the same. It's still very red. Good-night.'

As Frank was saying 'good-night' back, Flip managed to whisper to Bella, 'Have you ever heard of a bath that flies and squeaks and has to be caught in a bath towel?'

Bella barely had time to say, 'It's not a BATH. It's a bat!' before Frank closed the front door.

The terriers were now more confused than ever. Then Flip spoke without thinking. He said, 'Maybe we should ask Catriona in the morning.'

'Ask Catriona!' Flop was amazed. 'But she is a cat!'

Flip felt very ashamed. 'I'm sorry. I forgot!'

Frank looked at them. 'I suppose that the noise you are making means you'd like to go out and piddle before you go to bed.'

'Yes, please,' said Flip.

'Me too,' said Flop.

Frank went to get the leads. 'That was Mr. Rice to see that we were all right. He heard Mum scream. I explained what had happened. I'm going to take the dogs out for a few minutes.'

'Just don't let any bats into the house,' warned Mrs. Johnson.

'I won't. Don't worry!' Frank attached the leads to the dogs' collars, carefully opened and closed the front door and walked up the drive.

Bella was waiting for them at the gate. 'I didn't go back in when Mr. Rice left your place. There is something strange going on somewhere.'

'The cats are having a party at the hotel,' said Flip.

'Ah then, that explains the sounds. Listen! You'll be able to hear it too.'

Flip and Flop listened. In the distance, they could hear very strange singing. 'That won't last very long,' said Bella. 'The people who own the hotel will soon chase them away.'

Bella was right. By the time Frank and the dogs came back from their short walk, the singing had stopped.

'Good-night,' Bella said and ran to the front door of the Rices where she barked softly until she was let in.

In the Johnsons' house, Flip and Flop settled down in their basket. The moon looked in through the window. Later on so did a cat. But the dogs were fast asleep by then.

7
The Adventure by the Canal

Next day, at first light, Frank opened the door
of the dogs' room and looked in at them.
They had just wakened up. 'No noise now,'
he said. 'I've been tidying up my room. I
have two big bags of rubbish to take to the
dump. I thought we would go there now
before the sun is too hot. The two of you
could have a nice walk. Then we will come
back here and I can do some writing.'

Flip and Flop wagged their tails. It seemed
like a good idea for Frank to stay out of the
sun. His face looked a bit better but not very
much.

'No barking now,' he said as he went into
the hall and unlocked the hall door. His car
was where he had left it after the visit to
the vet. 'Good thing I didn't put it away.
I might wake Mum and Dad opening the
garage.'

Flip and Flop liked it when Frank talked
to them like this. Frank did it, not because
he thought that they could understand him,

but because he knew that the sound of his voice stopped the dogs barking.

He opened the back of the hatchback and put in two big plastic bags of rubbish, mainly things that had got broken when the cottage wall fell in. He had brought them home with the idea of getting them mended.

Then last night, not able to sleep because of the pain of his sunburn, he had looked at the things again and saw that they could not be fixed.

He had crept downstairs, got two rubbish bags and put the broken things into them.

Now he was ready to go for a nice drive down the country to a dump that he had seen a few months ago.

He closed the back of the hatchback.

'Where are we going to sit?' wondered Flip and Flop. They were usually put where the bags now were.

'You may sit on the back seat but only this once,' said Frank.

And so off they went. Flip and Flop found the back seat much more comfortable than being in their usual place. They didn't get bounced around so much. It was also very easy to see out of the window.

Being so early in the morning, there was

not much traffic about. Soon they left the city and drove along a fine wide road. Then they reached a town that was just wakening up to the new day. They drove down the main street. Then they turned right down the side of a big building and came out along a straight road by a stretch of bright shining water. A dog was nosing around a clump of grass.

Flip and Flop gave a slight bark when they saw him.

'Now, now,' said Frank. 'The world doesn't belong to you. Other animals are allowed to live in it as well.'

Flip and Flop thought this was a silly thing to say. Of course, other animals were allowed to live in the world! Flip and Flop had already met several of them.

Then they saw cows in a field. They did not interest Flip and Flop in the same way as the sheep up the mountains. They were too big and serious-looking. All the same, the dogs could not help but look back at them and keen.

'Don't worry,' Frank said. 'You'll soon be out of the car. Then you will be able to walk along the canal.'

Oh, so that was what the shining water

was called; a canal! It seemed to go on for ever. The fields on either side of it were very flat.

Then the dogs heard the sound of seagulls.

They propped themselves against the front seats and looked out through the windscreen. The sky ahead was full, not just of seagulls, but of many other birds too.

'Well, here we are!' Frank stopped the car. Behind a tall wire fence was a very interesting set of objects with a wonderful smell that reminded them of the dead bird on the beach. 'You stay here while I put the bags on the dump,' Frank said.

Oh, so this wonderful place was the 'dump'!

Frank took the plastic bags out of the car and threw them on the dump. The birds scattered out of his way. Then, as soon as he had driven off, they swooped back down.

Frank drove until he came to a ruined cottage. Here he stopped the car again and let the dogs out. They waited for him to put on their leads. Instead, Frank said, 'It's a fine straight road with no traffic this time of day. You can have a run without getting into trouble. Just take it nice and easy.'

And Flip and Flop did take it nice and easy

— at first. They snuffled and they sniffed and they ran from one side of the road to the other. They forgot about the dump and its smells.

Then suddenly they heard a sound like they had never heard before. It seemed to come on the morning breeze that blew across the fields.

Frank gave no sign that he heard anything. He was leaning against the car, thinking about his book.

Then the sound stopped.

The dogs stood, trembling, on the edge of the canal.

Then the sound began again. And it was calling to them. It was telling them that they had to obey.

Every other thought went from their heads. They jumped into the deep mud where the tall grasses and weeds grew along the edge of the canal. They pushed through the mud into the water and swam to the opposite bank. They climbed out of the mud there and set off across the countryside.

On and on they went until they came to a high wall. The sound was coming from behind the high wall.

They ran along by the wall until they came

to a metal gate with bars too close together for them to fit through. They could see big, spreading trees and green, mown grass. Beyond the trees was a huge house.

The sound seemed to get louder and louder. Then it stopped.

The dogs looked at each other, very puzzled. A dark shadow fell across them. They were caught by the scruffs of the neck. It was Frank and he was very angry.

He said, 'What do you two think you are doing? If a farmer saw you running like that across his land, he might think you were after his sheep!'

Then Frank became as puzzled as the dogs. 'But there *are* no sheep! In fact, apart from those cows that we passed a few miles back, there are no animals of any kind out on the land! Then, what made you run away? Did you hear something?'

Frank attached the leads to the dogs' collars and looked in through the gate. 'Was it something in there that you heard?'

The sound began again. Flip and Flop flung themselves at the gate. 'All right, all right,' Frank said. 'We'll have a look.' He opened the narrow gate.

Flip and Flop knew exactly where to go.

They led Frank to the driveway of the big house.

A man was lying on the drive. His face was twisted with pain. He had a whistle in his hand. 'Thank heavens,' he said. 'I'd almost given up hope of being found.'

'What happened?' Frank asked.

'I'm paid to keep an eye on this place while the owners are away. I decided to check it out early. I tripped. I think I've broken my ankle.'

Frank helped the man to sit up. 'That whistle that you have there, is it the kind that only dogs can hear?'

'It is. I use it to train my dog. I don't know

82

why he didn't come when I whistled. If you go through that green door there, you are almost in Innisdara. You can get help.'

Even as the man spoke, the green door opened. A boy and a girl and a black labrador came into the parkland. There were several other dogs behind them, which the children locked out.

In spite of his pain, the man managed to laugh. 'I spoke too soon. Not only is Darkie here but every dog for miles around. Like your two terriers, they must all have heard the whistle.'

Darkie said nothing to Flip and Flop until he was sure that the man was all right.

'These are the Maguire children,' the man said. 'They'll go and get help.'

The Maguire children rushed off to the town of Innisdara. Frank and the man talked about the big house. Flip said to Darkie, 'Where were you when the man fell?'

'In the lane chasing rabbits,' Darkie said. 'When he blew the whistle, I knew he needed help. I was lucky to meet Joe and Maeve Maguire. They knew at once that I wanted them to follow me.'

The green door opened again. The Maguires were back with their parents and the local doctor. 'I'll be fine now,' said the man to Frank. 'I'm sorry you had to run such a distance.'

'Luckily there was a bridge that I was able to cross instead of going through the canal. Otherwise, I'd be as smelly as these two.'

'The mud'll soon dry,' said the man.

Frank watched the man being helped to where the doctor's car was. Then he set off back to his car with Flip and Flop. Luckily, a fresh-water stream ran at the back of the ruined cottage close to where Frank had parked.

He dipped both terriers in it. 'That'll have to do until we get home,' he said. 'And at least you can go in your usual place and not on the back seat!'

He opened the hatchback. Flip and Flop jumped in, but Frank stood there for a few minutes, thinking. Then he said, 'Do you know something? I think what happened just now has given me an idea for an adventure story, about a black labrador and two children called Maguire.'

Flip and Flop felt cross. After all, they had been the ones that had started the adventure by running across the fields. If Frank was going to write a book about dogs, he should write one about them!

Frank grinned as though he knew what they were thinking. He said, 'And after the story of the black dog, I might write one about two border terriers from Scotland who came to live in Ireland!'

The dogs barked happily.

Then, Frank got into the car and drove away from the canal, and back to the house overlooking the sea.

8
Making Friends

Traffic was much heavier than when they'd driven out of the city. It took them a long time to get back to the house. Mr. Johnson's car was still parked by the garage.

'I hope nothing is wrong,' Frank said. 'Dad should have left for the office an hour ago.'

The dogs kept very close to Frank as, together, they went into the house. Mrs. Johnson came out of the kitchen as soon as she heard the living-room door open.

'Ah, there you are,' she said. 'We didn't hear you go out this morning.'

'Why is Dad still here?' asked Frank.

'Go and ask him yourself,' smiled Mrs. Johnson. 'He's outside in the garden. Breakfast will soon be ready. We can have it out on the terrace.'

Mr. Johnson was examining his rose-trees to see if there were any greenfly on them. He straightened up when he saw Frank.

'Oh, so you're back with the two brutes.'

Flip and Flop didn't like the way Mr.

Johnson looked at them when he said 'the two brutes', so they decided that they'd better keep out of his way. They made for the big bush at the bottom of the garden. They had hardly settled down there when Catriona appeared on top of the wall.

'Hello, boys', she said.

Flip and Flop ignored her. They were determined not to talk to her at all this morning. They were too worried about Mr. Johnson and the way he had looked at them. But not being spoken to didn't worry Catriona. She yawned and blinked at the sun, which was already quite warm.

'Excuse me for yawning,' she said. 'I'm so tired after the party at the hotel last night. The other cats insisted that I sing and sing and sing. In fact I might still be there if those silly humans at the hotel hadn't yelled so rudely at us. But still what can you expect? Have you ever listened to what *they* call singing?'

Then she realised that not only were the dogs not talking to her; they weren't even listening to her. They were too busy thinking about Mr. Johnson and Frank.

'Dear, oh dear,' murmured Catriona. 'I do so hope Frank isn't in more trouble with his father!'

In spite of not wanting to speak to her, Flop just could not let this remark pass unanswered. 'And since when have you cared what happens to Frank?'

'It's not Frank that I am worried about,' said Catriona. 'It's you and Flip. Whatever happens to Frank could be good or bad for the two of you. Shall I slip through the shrubs and listen to what is being said?'

Flip and Flop glanced at each other. It would be silly to refuse her offer of help just because she was a cat. And she *did* seem to mean it when she said that she cared what happened to them. They actually had a friend who was a cat!

'All right,' Flip said.

'Thank you very much,' said Flop.

'My pleasure,' purred Catriona, jumping down off the wall and landing on the ground without making even the smallest sound. Then she ran through the shrubs until she was close enough to the rose-trees to hear what Frank and Mr. Johnson were saying.

After listening for a few minutes, Catriona came back to the dogs.

'Frank was telling his father,' she announced, 'that he might get the book that he is writing finished today. So he will be going to London very soon. He can't take you with him until he finds a place to live.

'Mr. and Mrs. Johnson may also be going away soon — on a business trip. They don't know *what* to do about the two of you. I hope that Frank doesn't decide to give you away!'

Before Flip and Flop could even think of how terrible it would be to be given away, Mrs. Johnson came out on to the terrace and called out, 'Breakfast is nearly ready! And I have something special for Flip and Flop too!'

For almost the first time in their lives Flip and Flop did not feel hungry. All the same they followed Frank and Mr. Johnson up to the terrace. Mrs. Johnson put down two plates of brown bread and cooked bacon rind in a shady spot.

Then she noticed the sad look in the dogs' eyes. 'Are the dogs all right?' she said to Frank. 'They seem very quiet.'

'They are probably worn out after their adventure by the canal,' said Frank.

'What adventure was that?' asked Mr. Johnson.

While Frank helped his mother to carry the breakfast things out to the table on the terrace he told his parents what had happened at the canal. 'And later on, when I'm settled in London, I am going to write a book for young people, all about a labrador down by the canal.'

'That sounds like a good idea,' said Mrs. Johnson.

As they started to eat breakfast Frank said to his father, 'Are you not going into the office today?'

'No. Your mother and I had such a good time yesterday driving around that I have decided to take today off as well. There's not much going on in there anyway.' He gave a little smile. 'Did you think that I had stayed home just to talk to you?'

'Yes. That's exactly what I thought when I saw your car still outside,' said Frank.

'Well it wasn't just because of that, although I am glad that we had our chat.'

'What did you decide?' asked Mrs. Johnson.

'I'll be going to London soon,' replied Frank. 'Lucy will be back from America at the end of the month. Then she and I will have to make plans.'

'And what about Flip and Flop?'

'I don't think Dad wants them here a

second longer than they have to be,' said Frank.

Mr. Johnson sighed. 'Now you know perfectly well that your mother and I will be away ourselves. We can't leave the dogs here all alone.'

'We could always ask the Rices next door to look after them, or find someone in the village,' said Mrs. Johnson.

Frank shook his head. 'I suggested that. But Dad just doesn't like Flip and Flop.'

Mr. Johnson said, 'There is a reason why I don't like dogs. When I was six years old a dog attacked me for no reason. Luckily my father was with me and saved me from being bitten. I've tried to like dogs since then but somehow I just can't manage it.'

'But Flip and Flop would never attack you,' said Mrs. Johnson. 'They're the nicest little dogs I've ever known.'

Mr. Johnson looked at Flip and Flop. They tried to wag their tails at him. He said, 'Yes, I know they are nice dogs. In fact I suppose in a way I've got quite fond of them. But I don't feel as though I can trust them. Anyway, Frank should be getting on with his writing. He shouldn't be out in the sun either until his face is completely better.'

91

Frank, seeing that there was no point in talking any more that morning about Flip and Flop, began to clear the table. 'What will you and Mum do today?' he asked.

'Go for another drive,' said Mr. Johnson. 'I have the name of a nice place for lunch down in Wicklow. I put the directions in my wallet.' He stood up and reached into his back pocket. He looked puzzled.

'What's wrong?' Frank asked.

'I can't find my wallet!'

'Perhaps you left it in your other suit,' said Mrs. Johnson. 'Or on the dressing-table.'

Mr. Johnson hurried into the house. Frank and Mrs. Johnson put the breakfast things on a tray.

'Imagine a big man like Mr. Johnson being afraid of dogs!' whispered Flop to Flip. 'If only we could do something that would show him that we want to be really friendly.'

Then the dogs noticed Catriona down by the rose-bushes. She was bouncing up and down in the air. Her tail was waving like a flag on a windy day.

'What's the matter with her?' asked Flip.

Bella, who had just come through the gap in the hedge, was wondering the very same thing.

'Hey,' she asked, 'what's going on?'

'I've found Mr. Johnson's wallet,' said Catriona excitedly. 'It must have fallen out of his pocket when he bent down to look at the rose-trees. If Flip and Flop bring the wallet back to Mr. Johnson he will have to admit that not only are they nice dogs but that they are good, useful dogs too!'

'You are absolutely right!' said Bella and she dashed up the garden to explain the situation to Flip and Flop.

They at once followed Bella back down to the rose-bushes.

'One of you must pick up the wallet,' instructed Catriona. 'The other one must bark.'

Quick as a flash Flip took the wallet in his mouth. Flop ran back up the garden, barking.

Mr. Johnson was standing on the terrace. 'Stop the noise!' he yelled. 'I've lost my wallet! Your barking makes things worse!'

Then he saw the wallet in Flip's mouth.

He turned and called to Frank and Mrs. Johnson who were in the kitchen, 'Just come out and see what the dogs have done!'

Frank and Mrs. Johnson came rushing out, expecting bad news. 'What's wrong?'

'Nothing is wrong,' said Mr. Johnson. 'In fact everything is great, thanks to Flip and Flop!' He took the wallet from Flip. 'They've found my wallet! Good dogs! Do you know I think that you and I might become real friends after all.'

'Does that mean that they can stay here for a while when I go to London?' asked Frank.

'Yes, of course it does,' said Mr. Johnson. 'We can work something out for the times when your mother and I are away too.' He patted Flip and Flop. They licked his hand.

They they licked Frank's hand. And then Mrs. Johnson's hand.

Then they danced around the terrace with Bella.

They they remembered the dishes of bread and bacon rind.

'Come and eat it with us,' they said to Bella. 'And maybe we should give some to Catriona. After all, not only is she our friend but she helped us to make friends with Mr. Johnson too.'

But Catriona had gone from the garden as quietly as she had come into it.

'Never mind,' said Bella. 'She'll be back.'

When the dishes were empty the three dogs went and stretched out in the shade of the big bush.

They found it hard to imagine that there could be three happier dogs in the whole world.

Flip'n'Flop

Flip and Flop are two border terriers who have come all the way from Scotland to start a new life in the Wicklow Hills.

It's not hard to tell which is which! Flip is the one who is 'forever flipping around the place, trying to find out what things are about'. Flop is 'forever flopping over and wanting to sleep'.

Meet the two pups, their owner Frank (who has his own problems), their friend Beauty (the sheepdog), and their enemy Tomser (the cat).

The first Flip and Flop book is also illustrated by Maria Murray.

112 pages, illustrated. £2.95